III

THE TALKATIVE SPARROW

AND OTHER STORIES

This edition published in 2016 by Pikku Publishing
7 High Street
Barkway
Hertfordshire SG8 8EA
www.pikkupublishing.com

ISBN: 978-0-9934884-1-2

First published by the University of London Press Ltd in 1936

Pikku Publishing and Dr Frances Grundy, heir to the estate of
Elizabeth Clark, wish to state that they have used all reasonable
endeavours to establish copyright. If you would like to contact
the Publisher, please write to Pikku Publishing.

1 3 5 7 9 10 8 6 4 2

Printed in China by Toppan Leefung Printing Ltd

" TELL THE PRIME MINISTER TO *CATCH* THAT SPARROW,"
HE SAID.

(*See page* 13)

THE TALKATIVE SPARROW

AND OTHER STORIES

by
ELIZABETH CLARK

Author of "Twenty Tales for Telling,"
"Tales for Jack and Jane," etc.

Illustrated by
NINA K. BRISLEY

Pikku Publishing

AUTHOR'S NOTE

The tales in this little book and its companions are reprinted from various collections of stories for storytellers which I have written during the past ten years.

It has been very often suggested to me that children would enjoy reading these stories quite as much as (I am happy to believe) they have hitherto enjoyed hearing them read or told. Accordingly, some of the stories have been chosen.

I hope that these small books may bring pleasure to innumerable small people, at home, at school, or wherever they and the books may be.

ELIZABETH CLARK

CONTENTS

The TALE of the TALKATIVE SPARROW

Chapter One : Mrs. Sparrow's Treasure

ONCE upon a time a sparrow had her nest upon a great gateway that was the entrance to a King's palace. The gateway was of marble, and it was covered with wonderful carvings of battles and of Kings going hunting. It was like a picture-book of stories told in stone.

Under the gateway people came and went all day. There were the King's soldiers with their shining spears and swords and helmets. There were merchants bringing rich carpets and furs, and gold and silver and precious stones to sell to the King. There were ambassadors from far countries with their trains of servants, who came to bring gifts and talk about affairs of state, and there were people of the King's own country who came to tell their troubles and ask for help.

The sparrows looked down from their nests among the carvings and hopped and chirped and watched it all, and told each other in sparrow talk what they thought about it.

Sparrows are noisy birds, but one of these sparrows made more noise than any sparrow you ever met. She never stopped talking, and it was all about her own affairs. When any-one else tried to tell her a sparrow-story, she always chimed in and told one of her own instead. Very often everyone had heard that story so often that nobody wanted to hear it again, but nothing could stop her talking.

Just at the time this story begins all her sparrow-children had grown up and flown away. So she had plenty of time to talk. As for her sparrow-husband, no one knew where he was. Perhaps he had gone somewhere else, because she talked so fast and loud.

One day when Mrs. Sparrow was pecking and scratching in the road to see what she could find to eat, she saw something shining in the dust. It was only a piece of glass, but it sparkled so brightly that Mrs. Sparrow thought it must be something very wonderful. She picked it up in her little bill and carried it to her nest.

There she sat, fluttering with excitement and twittering very loudly.

" I have a treasure that is greater than the King's ! I have a treasure that is greater than the King's ! I have a treasure that is greater than the King's ! "

Her sparrow friends came crowding round to see the wonderful thing. They pushed and pecked and quarrelled and chirped. Their shrill little voices grew louder and louder, but above

them all could be heard Mrs. Sparrow, shrieking :

" I have a treasure that is greater than the King's."

It was really a terrible noise.

Chapter Two : The King is Angry

Now this happened just at noon-time, and in the country where Mrs. Sparrow lived, every-one rests in the middle of the day because the sun shines so hot and fiercely. The King lay on his bed in his great cool room ; he was just dozing off to sleep most comfortably, when the noise began. All the sparrows seemed to be chirping at once, and above them all he could hear one of them saying, " Cheep-cheep-*cheep* ! Cheep-cheep-cheep-cheep-*cheep* ! "

That of course was Mrs. Sparrow's voice. He listened for a little while and hoped they would soon be quiet ; but the noise grew louder. At last the King said very crossly :

" This is disgraceful. Tell the Prime Minister to find out what all the fuss is about."

They told the Prime Minister that the King could not sleep, and wished him to find out what made the sparrows so noisy.

" Tell the Lord High Chamberlain to attend to the matter at once," said the Prime Minister. He considered himself far too grand to be concerned with sparrows.

The Lord High Chamberlain told the Butler, and the Butler told the Cook, and the Cook told the Kitchen-boy.

The Kitchen-boy climbed up the great carved gateway, holding on to the carving with his fingers and toes. He put his hand into Mrs. Sparrow's nest and found the piece of glass. All the sparrows stopped chattering and flew away when they

saw him coming, except Mrs. Sparrow. She would not leave her treasure, but even she was quiet.

" Here is a fine treasure for the King," said the Kitchen-boy ; and he laughed and put the piece of glass in his mouth to keep it safe as he climbed down again. He gave it to the Cook, and the Cook gave it to the Butler, and the Butler gave it to the Lord High Chamberlain, and the Lord High Chamberlain took it to the Prime Minister, and the Prime Minister laid it on a golden tray and carried it to the King.

" This is what the sparrows were making a noise about, your Majesty," he said.

The King looked at it and said, " Take it away."

He spoke very crossly because he was very sleepy, and turned over on his other side and said to himself, " Now I shall have a little peace and quiet."

Then—would you believe it ?—the noise began again, worse than ever. Mrs. Sparrow had made up a poem about her piece of glass and was shrieking it at the top of her voice :

" The King has borrowed my shining treasure.
I lent it to him with pride and pleasure.
No doubt he will pay me back in good
measure."

It was all in sparrow talk, of course, and it
was not a good poem. But all the other
sparrows joined in. Some laughed, some
cheered, some chattered ; and the noise they
made was dreadful.

The King sat up, wide awake and very angry.

" Tell the Prime Minister to *catch* that
sparrow," he said.

So the Prime Minister sent for the Lord
High Chamberlain, and the Lord High Chamberlain sent for the Butler, and the Butler
told the Cook, and the Cook told the Kitchen-
boy. The Kitchen-boy climbed up the great
carved gateway once more, holding on with
his fingers and toes. He put out his hand and
caught Mrs. Sparrow, who was still sitting on
her nest saying her poem at the top of her voice.

" The King wants you," said the Kitchen-
boy. Then he held Mrs. Sparrow very tight

13

with one hand, and climbed carefully down the carved gateway.

Poor Mrs. Sparrow was nearly fainting with fright, but she felt very proud to think the King had sent for her, and she managed to call to her friends :

" The King has sent for me. I will get you all places at Court."

The Kitchen-boy carried her into the Palace and gave her to the Cook, and the Cook gave her to the Butler, and the Butler gave her to the Lord High Chamberlain, and the Lord High Chamberlain gave her to the Prime Minister. But just as the Prime Minister was going to take her to the King, poor little Mrs. Sparrow really did faint right away from fright.

The Prime Minister laid her on a gold and jewelled tray, like a dusty little bundle of brown feathers, and took her to the King.

" The Bird appears to be dead, your Majesty," he said very grandly.

The King said, " A very good thing too. Take it away and bury it. Now perhaps I can get a little sleep."

So the Prime Minister walked out again and said very grandly to the Lord High Chamberlain:

"Take the Bird and bury it." The Lord High Chamberlain told the Butler, and the Butler told the Cook, and the Cook told the Kitchen-boy; and the Kitchen-boy went out into the Palace garden and made a little hole and popped little Mrs. Sparrow into it and covered her up. Then he went back into the Palace, and everybody really did get some sleep.

Chapter Three : A Friend in Need

IT would have been all up with Mrs. Sparrow if it had not been for the Dog who trotted after the Kitchen-boy, wondering if he had anything that was good to eat. As soon as the Boy had gone, the Dog began to scratch, and he very soon uncovered Mrs. Sparrow. Just at that moment Mrs. Sparrow opened her little black eyes, and sneezed, and fluttered her little wings, and tried to fly. She found that instead of being in her own nest she was lying on the ground, with a big Dog looking at her as if he meant to eat her.

She was terribly frightened, but she was really a brave little bird, and a plan came into her little brown head. Instead of trying to get away, she began to talk.

" Oh, dear ! " said Mrs. Sparrow to the Dog. " Are you going to eat me ? "

" I certainly am," said the Dog.

" Dear me ! " said Mrs. Sparrow. " How sorry I am for you ! My feathers are quite full of dust from that nasty hole. I really think you had better wash me first."

" That seems a good idea," said the Dog. " I should never have thought of that."

So he carried Mrs. Sparrow to the basin of a

fountain, and held her in the water till the dust was all washed from her feathers. Poor little Mrs. Sparrow did not like it at all, but she bravely made no fuss.

" Are you going to eat me now ? " she said, when the Dog had finished.

" I certainly am," said the Dog.

" But I should taste so very nasty and wet," said Mrs. Sparrow. " Hadn't you better dry me first ? "

" That is a very good idea," said the Dog,

and he held Mrs. Sparrow carefully between his paws while the hot sun dried her brown feathers.

By and by Mrs. Sparrow gave a little cheep and fluffed herself as well as she could.

17

" I *think* I am quite dry now," she said. " But just let me flap my wings and see. It would be a pity to spoil the taste."

" Certainly it would," said the Dog, and he moved his paws.

Mrs. Sparrow flapped her wings. She flapped her wings and flew. Right up to the nest at the top of the great carved gateway she flew, and there she sat and never spoke a word. She had so much to think about.

All her friends knew what had happened. The pigeons that peeped in at the Palace windows had told them the first part, and the birds in the Palace garden had told them the rest. They were very glad to see her back safe and sound, but they really could not help laughing at her. Ever after, if she talked too importantly and too loudly somebody was quite sure to say softly:

" Did the King tell you that when you went to Court, or did the Dog whisper it in your ear in the Palace garden ? "

And that always made her feel very quiet.

THE TALE OF PETER PEREGRINE PATCH

Chapter One :

The Thief in the Night

PETER PEREGRINE PATCH was in trouble about his green peas. There had been a beautiful row of them in his garden, all ready for picking. Only the night before, Peter had looked at them and said, " I will pick them to-morrow. There must be quite a peck. With the money I shall get for them, and with what I have saved, I shall have enough to buy a new coat to be married in."

His real name was not Peter Peregrine *Patch*

at all. It was Peter Peregrine *Partington*, but everyone called him Patch because of his coat. Once upon a time it had been a blue coat, but now it was more like a very queer patch-work quilt.

Peter lived all alone, and he had no one to mend for him ; but he had a tidy mind and he could not bear holes. So whenever there was a hole in his coat he sewed on a patch with a few big stitches. Some of the patches were leather, and some were sacking ; some were green baize, and some were brown corduroy. There were even one or two of red flannel. It was a very odd coat, but it kept out the rain and the cold, and Peter did not mind being laughed at.

But now he was going to be married. He had worked and saved till his pigs and his chickens and his home and his garden were all ready and as neat as new pins. Then he had asked the girl he liked best to marry him. Her name was Prudence Priscilla. Prudence Priscilla said :

" Yes, but you must get a new coat to be married in."

That was why Peter was in trouble about his peas.

" I did want to get married on Monday, and now I can't," he was saying to himself.

There had been a beautiful row of peas only the night before. But by morning they were all gone, every one of them, and there was nothing to show how. There was not a foot-mark, not even a broken twig or a fallen leaf. Somebody had picked them. But who could it be ?

" There is a moon to-night," said Peter. " I shall sit by the window and watch. The next row will be ready to pick to-morrow, and I will take good care that is not stolen too."

Chapter Two : The Wise Woman

PETER sat all night by the window, watching, but there was never a sound in the garden. Not a leaf rustled. Nothing and nobody stirred. But when morning came there was not a pea left on the second row ; and so it was on the third and fourth nights too. Peter watched by the window. He heard nothing, he saw nothing, but the peas were gone.

Next night would be full moon, and there was still one row of peas left, and a very fine row too. That day Prudence Priscilla had a bright idea—for of course Peter had told her all about his trouble.

" Go and ask the Wise Woman," she said. " If only you can gather this row of peas and take them to market to-morrow, you will still be able to buy your new coat, and we can be married on Monday just the same."

Peter thought it was a bright idea too, so off he went and told the Wise Woman.

" Ha-hem-hum," said she. " When I was a girl I heard my grandmother, who was a Wise Woman too, talk of something just like this. Let me think, Peter."

Peter sat very quiet in the Wise Woman's kitchen while the Wise Woman thought. The clock ticked and the fire flickered. Once or twice a cinder fell into the ashes ; but the Wise Woman never moved for a whole hour. At the end of that time she spoke.

" Yes, Peter," she said, " I remember sure enough. Come to me at nine o'clock to-night, when the moon rises and the sun sets, and I will tell you what to do."

Peter went to Priscilla's home and told her what the Wise Woman had said, and at nine o'clock that night he tapped at the Wise Woman's door. But no one came to answer it. He was just wondering if it would be polite to knock again, when the Wise Woman put her head out of the little window that looked out of her roof. She had a frilled night-cap on her silvery head,  and in her hand she held a little packet.

23

" There you are, Peter," she said, throwing the packet down to him. " There are twenty-four hairs. I pulled twelve from each side of my head. Take them, join them together, and fasten them round about the pea-row, just as high as your hand from the ground. When midnight strikes, you will see what you will see. Good night, Peter."

Without another word the Wise Woman pulled her head in and shut the window, and Peter had no more chance to ask her any questions.

" Thank you, ma'am," he said politely, and took off his hat, for he hoped she was watching from behind the curtain and would see that he was truly grateful. Then he picked up the little packet and went home.

There were twenty-four hairs in it, as the Wise Woman had said. Each of them was nearly a yard long, and all were shining silver-grey. They were very fine, but very strong. Peter knotted them together, and fastened them cleverly to little bits of stick stuck here and there, just as high as his hand, till there was a silvery line of hair all the way round the pea-row. In the silvery moonlight it could hardly be seen at all.

" And now," said Peter, " I will wait behind the old apple tree to see what I shall see when it strikes twelve o'clock."

Peter waited. It was eleven o'clock by that time, and the full moon was high in the sky. The pinks in the border by the path were shining white, and smelling even sweeter than by day, but everything else in the garden seemed fast asleep.

Peter was beginning to feel very sleepy himself when he heard the church clock strike twelve.

One—two—three—four—five—six—seven—eight—nine—ten—eleven—twelve !

Chapter Three : What Happened at Midnight

THE chimes sounded very loud in the stillness. Peter opened his eyes and felt very wide awake. As the twelfth stroke sounded, he saw the line of silver-grey hair shake gently all along its

25

length. Then, suddenly, a shower of little pointed red things, shaped just like the caps that some flowers wear when they are buds, fell on the ground. And there, before Peter's eyes, were dozens of tiny bare-headed little men all in green, tumbling helter-skelter over the hair. It was as thick as a rope to them, but as it was silvery they had never noticed it in the moonlight.

"Bless me!" said Peter. "It is the Pixies. The thieving monkeys! To think I never knew it!"

As he spoke he popped his hat down on a dozen of the little men with one hand, and with the other he gathered up all the red caps that he could reach. For Peter knew that no one can see a Pixy as long as he wears his cap, and he did not mean them to put on their caps and vanish from his sight.

Peter's hat had a large hole in the crown. Peter said it was to keep his head cool, but Priscilla said it was just a hole. He peeped in and saw the Pixies sitting on the ground weeping pixy tears. He felt very sorry for them, but he thought of his wedding and his coat and his peas.

All the other Pixies came crowding round, some crying for their caps, some begging him to let the little men under his hat go free. They all talked at once. They pulled at his coat. They patted his hands. They ran up his coat sleeve and whispered in his ear.

" Peter, Peter, Peter," they said, and it sounded like the little soft twitterings that birds make at break of day on a summer morning.

Peter shook his head because their whispering tickled.

" You little thieving monkeys ! " he said. " Run away, every one of you, and bring me enough to pay for the peas you have stolen, and you and your caps shall all go free before sunrise."

27

Away scurried the Pixies. In a minute the
garden was empty, except for Peter, and the
Pixies under his hat, and the flowers in the
moonlight. In no time at all they were back
again, and each one carried a little lump of
gold just the size and shape of a fat green pea.
They piled them before Peter in a little shining
yellow heap.

" Thank you, kind neighbours," said Peter.
" The bill is very well paid."

Then he picked up his hat and dropped the
caps, and the next moment there was not a
Pixy to be seen. Peter thought he could hear
tiny twittering voices crying, " Good day.

28

HE BOUGHT A FINE NEW COAT.

Peter. Good day. Good day." But it might have been just a sleepy bird calling from its nest in the hedge. He never could be quite sure whether it was the Pixies or not: they vanished so quickly and quietly from sight.

Peter picked up the golden peas and put them in his pocket. Then he went into his house and fell fast asleep in his kitchen arm-chair.

When the sun was up, Peter woke up too, and washed his face, and brushed his hair, and went to market. But it was gold peas, not green peas, that he took with him to sell. He sold them to the goldsmith for quite a pile of gold pieces. He bought a fine new coat, and a gold-laced hat, and a most beautiful gold ring to put on Prudence Priscilla's finger. He gave a gold piece to the Wise Woman for every single hair: twenty-four gold pieces. There was still a pile of gold left when he had done all that.

So Prudence Priscilla and Peter Peregrine were married and lived happily ever after. Prudence Priscilla mended everything so neatly that no one ever dreamed of calling Peter anything but Peter Peregrine Partington. They quite forgot they had ever called him Peter Peregrine Patch.

As for his garden, it blossomed and bore so well that everyone said the Pixies must be keeping an eye on it. Perhaps they were, to make up for the time when Peter Peregrine Patch was in trouble about his peas.

THE SPINDLE,
THE SHUTTLE,
AND THE
NEEDLE

Chapter One : Rose-Marie

IN a little village on the edge of a great forest there lived a girl named Rose-Marie, who was just as pretty and as pleasant as her name. Her father and mother had died while she was only a little child, and then she lived with her old godmother, who loved her dearly.

The old woman had earned her living by spinning, weaving, and sewing, and she taught Rose-Marie to do the same. When she died she had no money to give her goddaughter, but she left her the little house, the spindle, the shuttle, and the needle, with one piece of advice :

" Keep all bright and busy, my child. Speak the truth, and love your neighbours, and all will be well."

Rose-Marie gave her promise and kept it. Though she lived all alone in her little house in the shade of a great lime tree outside the village, she was always bright and busy, helping her neighbours, sweeping and cleaning her house, spinning, weaving, or sewing. As she worked she sang the songs her godmother had taught her. The sun shone in at her window, the birds chirped among the branches of the tall lime tree, and rabbits and hares and little wood-mice frisked and played at the edge of the forest. Rose-Marie loved them all, and was very happy all day long. And though she was certainly poor, the wonderful thing was that there was always enough for her, and something over to give away.

Now there came a time when the king's son was old enough to marry. In those days kings' sons used to travel through the world looking for someone who would be just the wife they wanted ; so this prince set out on his journey like all the rest.

" I will only marry the maid who is both the richest and the poorest," he said ; and though he knew very well what he meant, nobody else could understand it at all.

In every town and village all the girls put on their very finest clothes, to look rich, and began to tell everyone how well they could keep house on a very little money, to sound poor. They all looked pretty, but none of them pleased the prince.

Presently he came to the village where Rose-Marie lived.

Now in that village there lived a girl who was very rich and very pretty. When she heard the prince was coming she said to herself, " He is quite certain to choose me."

So she put on all her very best clothes, a beautiful flounced skirt of rose-red silk, a green satin kirtle, a gold chain round her pretty white neck, and gold pins in her shining golden hair. Then she sat herself down on the bench beside her father's door to wait.

When the prince came riding down the street she rose up and made him the most beautiful curtsy that ever was seen. Down and down and down she went. Her rose-coloured silken skirt spread in fluffs and frills and flounces round her, till she looked like a great red rose.

The prince smiled and leaned from his saddle and threw her a kiss—she was so very pretty. He also swept off his cap with its long white feather, and made her a low bow for politeness' sake after her lovely curtsy.

Then he rode on down the street.

The rich man's daughter came slowly up out of her curtsy. She was very surprised. She sat down on the bench by the door of her father's house and said, " Well, I never did."

She had been sure the prince would stop and say, " Will you marry me ? "

But the prince rode on down the street and called to the people of the village.

" I have seen the richest maid of your village. Now show me the poorest."

" She lives in the little house under the great lime tree," they said. " Her name is Rose-Marie."

A little girl said, " She has a grey hen and she gave me one of its eggs."

A little boy said, " She helped me find my ball when I lost it."

A woman said, " She helped me with my spinning when I hurt my hand."

The prince smiled.

" She has enough and to spare ! " he said.

Now Rose-Marie was spinning and singing to herself as she spun. She was sitting by her window, because she hoped to see the prince ride by. But when she heard the sound of his horse's hoofs she stopped singing. She thought it was not respectful to a prince, and she was far too shy to look up.

Chapter Two : The Prince Rides By

THE prince rode slowly by. He looked at Rose-Marie and hoped she would look at him. But Rose-Marie only spun faster and faster, and never once looked out of the window. So the prince rode on down the road, and Rose-Marie began her song again. It was an old song of her godmother's :

" Spindle, spindle, haste, I pray ;
    Guide my true love's steps this way."

No sooner had she said it than the spindle hopped from the wheel and on to the window-ledge. Next moment it was on the ground, and with one long hop after another it went down the road with the linen thread trailing after it, shin-ing like gold in the sunshine.

There was no more spinning to be done without a spindle, so Rose-Marie took the shuttle and began to weave. As she wove, she sang another of her godmother's songs :

" Shuttle, shuttle, swift and smooth,
    Weave a carpet for my love."

But as soon as she had sung that far, the shuttle sprang from her hand and began to weave by itself. It worked so busily that in almost no time at all it was making a most wonderful carpet. The border was of roses and lilies, the centre was as golden as sunlight, and woven into the gold was a great green tree. On the tree were gay-coloured birds, and under it were tall stags, little hares and rabbits, and squirrels with bushy tails. It was a most beautiful carpet.

As the shuttle was so busy all by itself, there was nothing for Rose-Marie to do but to take the needle and sew a seam ; and as she sewed she sang another song her mother had taught her :

> " Needle, needle, sharp and fine,
>   Help to deck this house of mine."

She had sewn only a very little of her seam when she heard a rustling among the leaves of the great lime tree, and something floated softly in at her window. Rose-Marie looked up.

The needle twitched itself out of her hand, and the next moment it was sewing busily at a heap of soft green silk, just the colour of lime leaves, that lay upon the floor.

It was like a little streak of sunshine flashing, and it must have been threaded with sunlight, for it made gold stitches as it went.

Then two green curtains fluttered up, as if they were wings, and hung themselves at the window ; and when Rose-Marie had stopped looking at them in great surprise she was just in time to see a big soft green cushion float, almost as lightly as a soap-bubble, into the big wooden chair in which her godmother used to sit.

Then the beautiful carpet spread itself upon the floor, and Rose-Marie in her old everyday clothes stood wondering at it all.

She was wondering so much that she never heard the sound of hoofs, and she was most surprised of all when the prince stood in the doorway with her shuttle in his hand.

" Rose-Marie, Rose-Marie," he said, " I have brought you back your shuttle. Will you marry me ? "

Rose-Marie looked at him, and liked him. She curtsied right down to the beautiful carpet, and said, " Yes, with all my heart ! "

So they were married and lived happily ever after. Rose-Marie taught all her little girls to spin and weave and sew with her godmother's spindle and shuttle and needle. Many and many a time, too, she told her boys and girls the story of the wonderful things they did ; and the story always ended with her godmother's advice : " Keep bright and busy, speak the truth, and love your neighbours, and all will go well."

So no doubt they all lived happily ever after.

SO THEY WERE MARRIED.

THE STORY OF MOTHER FOX & THE TIGER

Chapter One : The Cubs

FATHER FOX and Mother Fox lived in a burrow among some bushes on the edge of the forest. Father Fox was a very fine fellow with a sharp nose, a silky coat, bright eyes and a bushy tail. Mother Fox was not quite so big as Father Fox, but just as handsome and much nicer.

To tell the truth, Father Fox was rather vain. He had a great opinion of his own cleverness, and none at all of Mother Fox's. Whenever they argued about anything it always ended in Father Fox saying:

" My dear, you mind the children and I will do the rest. Remember, Mother Fox, *I* have enough cleverness to fill a whole cart, but *you* have only enough to fill a very small basket ! "

Father Fox and Mother Fox had five beautiful fox cubs. They had silky coats, sharp noses, bright eyes, and bushy tails.

" They are very handsome cubs, my dear," Father Fox would say. " I cannot make up my mind how many are like me and how many are like you. To tell the truth, they are all so clever and so beautiful that I think they must all take after me."

Mother Fox did not think that was very nice of him, and she did not quite agree with him ; but she knew what he would say if she argued. So she said nothing at all to him, and only thought to herself, " They are the most beautiful fox cubs in the world." That was all that really mattered.

They were very hungry fox cubs. Father Fox and Mother Fox had to work very hard at getting food for them.

Not far away there was a village, and every night, when the people of the village were fast asleep, Father and Mother Fox used to creep out of their hole and prowl round to see what they could find. Sometimes they found scraps and bones that had been thrown away. Sometimes they stole chickens. They always came back with something. They had to go very quietly, for fear the dogs in the village should wake up and chase them. Besides, there were wolves and tigers prowling about by night, all quite ready to eat up Father Fox and Mother Fox if they could catch them.

One night they were coming back from the village. They had both been hunting very busily, and Father Fox thought that his share of food was much larger and finer than Mother Fox's. He was so proud of it that he could not stop talking. His voice got louder and louder, till Mother Fox grew quite worried.

" Father Fox," she said, " if you talk so loud the Tiger will hear you, and then what will become of us and the dear children's breakfast ? "

" Don't be so silly, my dear," said Father

Fox. " If the Tiger does hear, I am far too clever to let him catch us. Remember, *I* have enough cleverness to fill a very large cart, but *you* have only enough cleverness to fill a very small basket ! "

Just as he said that, someone laughed close

by in the darkness. It was not at all a nice laugh. It was too much like a growl.

" Well, Father Fox," a voice said, " here I am, all ready to eat you and Mother Fox for my supper, unless out of your cartload of cleverness you manage to stop me ! "

And out from behind a bush walked a large black and yellow striped tiger.

44

Chapter Two : Tiger !

THAT was a dreadful moment for Father Fox. He was terribly surprised and frightened. He simply could not find a single word to say, or think of a single thing to do, in spite of all his cartload of cleverness. He would have liked to run away, but he knew that was no use. However fast he ran, the tiger could catch him in two jumps. So he stood still and shook with fright. Poor Father Fox !

Then—he could hardly believe it—he heard Mother Fox speaking quietly.

" Oh, Uncle," she said, " how lucky that we met ! There is a question that greatly puzzles my husband and me ; but one so wise as you can surely answer it for us."

Now the tiger was very vain, and to be called 'Uncle' in his country is most respectful. He liked that, and he liked to be called wise too. So he said in a purring voice, " No doubt I can help you. Before I eat you up, tell me your question, and I will answer it."

" Well, Uncle," said Mother Fox, " my

husband and I have five beautiful cubs. We cannot agree which are most like my husband and which are most like me. But if one so wise as yourself looked at them he could tell at once. Will you do us this great honour?"

The tiger was very pleased. He said to himself, "I shall have foolish Father Fox and silly Mother Fox for my supper, and five fat cubs as well!"

So he answered very kindly, "Lead the way to your hole. Show me the cubs, and I will settle the whole matter."

"We will, Uncle, we will," said Mother Fox, as if she did not know what he meant to do.

She and Father Fox trotted in front, and the

tiger came prowling after. At last they came to the burrow.

"Father Fox," said brave Mother Fox, "go

down the hole and tell the dear children of the great honour our kind Uncle Tiger is going to show them."

" Be quick," growled the tiger.

Father Fox *was* quick! He popped into the burrow and was gone like a flash. Mother Fox and the tiger waited by the hole.

Father Fox was quick to go in, but he was not at all quick to come out. They waited a very long time, but nobody came—no Father Fox, no beautiful fat fox cubs. The tiger got more and more angry. He was tired of waiting and he wanted his supper.

" Where are your husband and the cubs ? " he roared.

" Uncle," said Mother Fox, " if you will excuse me, I will go and see."

47

" Tell them to be *quick*," growled the tiger.

" Yes, Uncle," said Mother Fox respectfully, and she popped into the burrow and was gone in a minute, while the tiger sat and waited by the hole.

Chapter Three : Mother Fox Wins

THE time went by. It seemed to the tiger a very long time indeed. It was getting near dawn, which is a tiger's bedtime, and he was terribly hungry. He was beginning to feel very angry indeed with Father and Mother Fox for keeping him waiting like this, when he heard a noise in the burrow and a little bark,

and saw Mother Fox's wise little head and bright eyes peeping at him.

" Oh, Uncle," said Mother Fox, " after all, we need not have troubled you. Father Fox

48

has settled the question. He says his beautiful and clever cubs are exactly like his beautiful and clever wife. Is he not a good kind husband ? " The tiger gave one angry snarl and clawed with his big paw at the mouth of the burrow. But Mother Fox was too quick.

" Good-bye, Uncle," she said.

Her bright eyes shone in the dark. She wrinkled up her sharp nose, and laughed, and whisked down the hole, and was gone. She was quite safe with Father Fox and the fat fox cubs. There was nothing left for the tiger to do but to go home to bed without any supper.

As for Father Fox and Mother Fox and the five fox cubs, they were all very happy. Father Fox stopped being quite so proud of himself, and was proud of his wife instead.

" I have a wise and beautiful wife, and five beautiful children just like her. How fortunate I am ! " he said.

THE OLD WOMAN, THE PIXIES, AND THE TULIPS

Chapter One : May-time

ONCE upon a time there was an Old Woman who lived in a little white house with a little window on each side of the door, and two more little windows looking out of the roof. There was a garden in front of the little house, and it was always full of flowers.

The Old Woman liked to have flowers all the year round, and she loved every one of them. Very early indeed, just after Christmas, there were snowdrops and yellow aconites and crocuses, and then primroses and violets and periwinkles, and presently daffydowndillies, wallflowers, pansies and forget-me-nots, and by and by pink-and-white daisies, roses, pinks, stocks and Canterbury bells and sweet-Williams, and after them asters, dahlias and Michaelmas daisies. Then it was Christmas again.

But the flowers that the Old Woman loved best of all were the tulips. They grew on each side of the little path that led up to her door, and quite early in April the Old Woman would begin to look for them. She used to walk up the path and down the path looking at the garden bed, till one day she would see a little green shoot. " There's one," she would nod her head and say.

Soon there would be another, and another and another and another, all up and down both sides of the path.

The Old Woman would walk up the path and down the path and watch them grow. The sun shone, the rain rained, and the wind blew soft, and the little green shoots grew taller and taller, and opened into green leaves with a flower-bud between them.

By and by the buds began to turn colour. Some were pink and some were white, some were yellow and some were red, and some were red and yellow. They grew tall and strong, and when they were all in bloom the Old Woman used to walk up the path and down the path between the rows of tulips, and she would say:

"All a-growing and a-blowing. So they be. All a-growing and a-blowing."

She thought they were very pretty indeed, and so they were.

One year it was May-time and the tulips were all in bloom. They were prettier than ever that year, tall and strong and fine. One night in May there was a full moon, a large round beautiful moon that made it almost as bright as day. It was really the Old Woman's bed-time, but just as she was going up to bed she thought of the tulips and how pretty they would look in the moonlight. She said to herself:

"I must just take one peep at them before I go to bed."

So she opened the door and peeped out. There stood the tulips, tall and beautiful in the moonlight. It was as light as day. There was a little wind blowing and the tulips were swaying to and fro, to and fro.

" All a-growing and a-blowing. All a-growing and a-blowing, so they be," said the Old Woman.

But it really was her bed-time, and she was just going to shut the door and go to bed, when all of a sudden she put her hand to her ear and listened.

Chapter Two : Music in the Night

" OH ! " said the Old Woman. " I can hear music, very sweet music. What can it be ? "

There was no other house near, and it was too late for anyone to be going by singing or whistling.

" What can it be ? " said the Old Woman again.

Instead of going to bed, she began to walk

down the path between the rows of tulips. The music was so sweet she felt she must get nearer. When she came to her little gate and leaned over it she could still see nobody, but the music sounded very near and clear and sweet.

All of a sudden the Old Woman said, " I know ! It is the pixies."

She remembered that just over the hedge, beyond her gate, there lay a pixy-ring, and she knew that when the moon shines bright in May-time the pixies come up from their homes underground to dance on the pixy-rings. It was their music she had heard. No wonder it sounded sweet.

But the Old Woman also knew that pixies do not like to be watched when they are dancing, so she didn't look over the hedge. She said :

" Bless their little hearts ! " and turned round to walk up the path between the rows of tulips. It really was time for her to go to bed !

But the tulips looked so pretty in the moonlight that the Old Woman felt she wanted to look a little closer. So she stooped down

quite close to a tulip—and then she gave a little jump.

"Why, bless me!" she said, and she peeped into the next tulip.

"Bless me!" she said again.

She peeped into the next, and the next, and the next and the next and the next, and each time she whispered, "Bless *me*!"

She went up the row and down the row. She peeped into every tulip. She was most surprised, and no wonder, for in every tulip there was a pixy baby, and it was fast asleep.

The Old Woman guessed what had happened. The pixies had come up from their homes underground to dance. They could not leave the babies behind—nobody could. And they could not dance with babies in their arms— nobody could. So they had thought of the tulips in the Old Woman's garden, and every pixy mother had tucked her baby up in a tulip-cradle. The tulips made beautiful cradles, so deep and safe, and the wind rocking them made all the pixy babies fall fast asleep.

The Old Woman was as pleased as could be. She said, " Bless their little hearts ! " a great

IN MAY-TIME THE PIXIES COME UP FROM THEIR HOMES
UNDERGROUND TO DANCE.

many times, and then she remembered it really was her bed-time and she went to bed.

But next night, and the night after, and the night after that, and every night when it was moonlight in May-time, the Old Woman always came and peeped ; and she always found the pixy babies asleep in the tulip-cradles.

Chapter Three : What Came Next

Now for a long time the Old Woman lived in the little white house. But after a very long time indeed the Old Woman did not live there any longer. Another person came to live there ; and, do you know, she didn't like flowers !

She said they wasted a deal of good ground that might be used for vegetables. So she pulled them up.

She pulled up the snowdrops and aconites and crocuses, the primroses and periwinkles, the daffydowndillies, wallflowers, pansies and forget-me-nots, the pink-and-white daisies and roses and pinks, the stocks and sweet-Williams and Canterbury bells, and the dahlias and asters and Michaelmas daisies.

She even pulled up the tulips.

She threw them all out on to the rubbish heap and planted the garden with vegetables in nice neat rows : carrots and onions, turnips and parsnips, cabbages and potatoes and peas. Where the tulips used to grow on both sides of the little path, she planted a row of parsley.

Now, in those days parsley was a very nice neat little plant, but it had no crinkles in its leaves. They were quite smooth and flat.

May-time came, and the full moon came, and the pixies came from their homes underground to dance on the pixy-ring. They brought their babies with them, and every pixy mother said to every pixy father, " My dear, we must tuck Baby up first."

So off they came to the garden to find the tulip cradles. But oh dear, oh dear—there weren't any tulip-cradles !

The pixy mothers were very angry indeed. Each one popped her baby down on the garden path and flew at the parsley and pinched it. They would have liked to pinch the person who had planted it where the tulips ought to be, but as they could not get at her they pinched the parsley. They

pinched it so hard that it has never come unpinched, and if you look at it you will see that it is all crinkly along the edges to this very day.

Then the pixies went to look for the tulips, and they found the poor things trying to grow on the dust-heap, but there were no tulip-cradles that year. So the pixies took the tulips, and all the other poor flowers as well, and planted them in a safe place. Next year when Maytime came, and the full moon came, there were the tulip-cradles all a-growing and a-blowing, and the pixies put their babies to sleep in them.

And they say—you can try for yourself and see that this is true—that some tulips smell a great deal sweeter than others. Those are the tulips that grew from the tulips that grew in the Old Woman's garden, where the pixies put their babies to sleep.

QUESTIONS

THE TALE OF THE TALKATIVE SPARROW (page 7)

1. Pretend that you have seen the gateway. Say what it is like.

2. In some ways Mrs. Sparrow was silly. How? In some ways she was sharp. How?

3. How would you know, even without the pictures, that the story did not happen in England?

4. Look at the pictures and say what kind of clothes were worn in that country by fine gentlemen and by humble boys.

5. Birds often build in queer places. You could tell some stories about that.

6. Make a little play showing how the King could not sleep and the Kitchen-boy was sent to see what was the matter. First he got the glass, then the sparrow. To end with, pretend that he saw the dog part and told the King about it.

THE TALE OF PETER PEREGRINE PATCH (page 19)

1. What was Peter Peregrine Patch's real name? Why did people call him what they did?

2. Taken all together, his three names are funny. Why? Make up some more names like that. See that they swing well.

3. Why was Peter particularly anxious for a good crop?

4. What did the Wise Woman give Peter? What did he do with them? Their colour made them particularly useful for the purpose. How?

5. How do the pictures show that this story must have happened quite a long time ago? Tell how Peter was dressed for his wedding.

6. Draw the part of the Wise Woman's house that the picture shows, and put on the rest.

61

THE SPINDLE, THE SHUTTLE, AND THE NEEDLE (page 31)

1. With whom did Rose-Marie live at first, and how did she make a living?

2. Was the house shady? How do you know?

3. Who made the carpet? Tell what it was like, or paint a picture of it.

4. What did the needle make?

5. Make up a piece about what the spindle did after it jumped out of the window.

6. Tell how fine ladies and gentlemen dressed in those days.

THE STORY OF MOTHER FOX AND THE TIGER (page 41)

1. What was Father Fox always saying? What do you think he changed it to at the end of the story?

2. How many cubs were there, and what were they like?

3. Why could the story not have happened in England? Where might it have happened?

4. Which of the animals might have said, " It pays to be polite "? How do you know?

5. Explain Mother Fox's clever plan.

THE OLD WOMAN, THE PIXIES, AND THE TULIPS (page 50)

1. Write down some of the flowers in the Old Woman's garden. Make a mark against those you know by sight.

2. Was the Old Woman's house one in a row? How do you know?

3. The Other Person was rather like someone else in this book. Who—and how?

4. Why, does it say, is parsley crinkled, and why do some tulips smell so sweetly?

5. Draw the Old Woman's house as prettily as you can.

6. Say what kind of things she wore.